MANDY AND THE PURPLE SPOTTED HANKY

Vivian French
Illustrated by Chris Fisher

Young Lions
an Imprint of HarperCollinsPublishers

First published in Great Britain in Young Lions in 1993 .
1 3 5 7 9 20 8 6 4 2

Lions is an imprint of HarperCollins Children's Books,
part of HarperCollins Publishers Ltd, 77-85 Fulham Palace Road,
Hammersmith, London W6 8JB

ISBN 0 00 674660 8

Printed and bound in Great Britain
by HarperCollins Book Manufacturing Ltd, Glasgow

Mandy was sitting up in bed and staring out of the window. Her eyes were sore, her nose kept running and her head felt as if it was full of cotton wool. She was fed up and miserable and sorry for herself.

The worst of it was that she usually felt very happy. When she was out with the gang she was always the best tempered, and she never *ever* cried...and here she was snuffling into her hanky and feeling as if she was about to burst into tears all the time.

"Perhaps I'm getting like Josie," she thought.

The door crashed open and Josie
came marching in.

"What do you want?" Mandy
asked crossly.

"It's my bedroom too, so you
can't keep me out." Josie stuck out
her tongue at Mandy, and went to
her toy drawer. She pulled it open
with a bang and sat down beside
it.

I'm going to play with my dollies

Mandy groaned. "Can't you go and play downstairs?"

"Why should I?" Josie picked up a battered teddy and waved him in the air. "B'rrrrrrm! B'rrrrrrm! Here comes Super Ted!"

She threw him across the room

and he landed on Mandy's bedside table, knocking over a glass of water.

JOSIE! LOOK WHAT YOU'VE DONE!

"Wasn't me," Josie said, pulling a doll out of the drawer. "It was teddy."

Mandy mopped at the spreading pool of water with a handful of paper hankies. "It was you, and it's a mess. Go and get a cloth."

"No !" said Josie, and she turned her back on Mandy.

Mandy glared at the back of her little sister's head, heaved herself out of bed and headed for the door.

As she went past Josie she tweaked one of Josie's little plaits.

Josie let out a loud and furious shriek. She jumped to her feet and pushed past Mandy to the top of the stairs.

"MUM! MUM!" she shrieked.

Mum came out
of the kitchen
wiping her hands.

"Can't you two be quiet for two
minutes?" she asked. "Mandy, I
thought I told you to stay in bed."

"Josie wants to play up here,"
Mandy said. "Can't I come down
just for a little while?"

Her mum sighed. "Wrap yourself
up warm, then," she said. "Look -
here's Grandad's cardigan. Put it on
or you'll be catching something
much worse than a cold. Now,
Josie, what are you going to do?"

Josie came down a couple of
steps.

"Can I keep Mandy company?"
she asked. "I'll be very good and
quiet."

"NO!" said Mandy. "If you're
coming downstairs I'm going back
to bed."

Josie looked at her mum and
then at Mandy. Mandy looked very
cross indeed, and Josie wasn't sure
that her mum looked very friendly.

"I'll play upstairs,"
she said, and
skipped off.

The doorbell rang. Josie, at the top of the stairs, stopped to see who it was. Mandy's mum opened the door, and Kevin,

Kim

and Ian

piled into the hallway followed by Buster.

"YUCK," said Josie loudly. "It's the horrible Staple Street gang." She giggled, and rushed into the bedroom.

Mandy's mum folded her arms. "If you've come to see Mandy you can have just half an hour," she said. "And then it's out - and mind you keep that dog off my furniture." She went into the kitchen banging the door behind her.

Mandy took the gang into the sitting room. They sat uneasily on the edges of the chairs and looked at each other.

They always felt happiest when they were all together out of doors, usually down at the square. Inside there were too many grown-ups who disapproved of them, although Mandy's mum was usually one of the friendliest. The problem with her was that she could never understand why they didn't want Josie tagging along as well.

Kevin's mum was just the same, and Kim's gran was always asking Josie to come for tea or to make buns or generally to get in the way.

Ian's mum had once made Ian stay in all day and play snakes and ladders with Josie. It was this peculiar behaviour by the grown-ups that had made the four friends think of being a gang – the "Let's Escape From Josie" gang.

"What have you all been doing?" Mandy asked, and sneezed loudly.

"Nothing much," said Kevin. "Buster got fleas, so even when my cold was worse than anyone's Pete made me go out and brush him with flea powder.

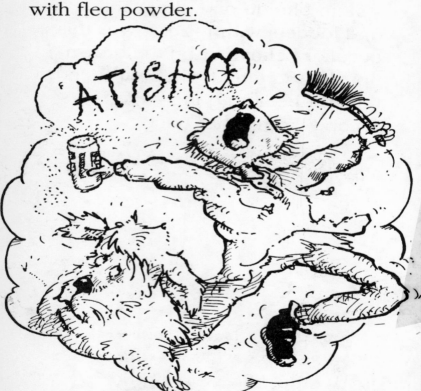

Oh, and I came next-but-last in the relay in the swimming gala."

"My cold was worse than yours,"
Ian said indignantly. "I sneezed
through packets and packets of
paper hankies. I nearly wasn't
allowed to go swimming at all."

"Serves you right," Kim said.
"You gave us all colds after you
had yours. Mine was horrid."

"I did NOT!" Ian said. "Colds just
happen."

"No they don't," Mandy said. "I didn't have a cold at all till you lot sneezed all over me. And then I had to go to bed and miss the swimming gala altogether. And everyone knows I might have won the backstroke."

Her eyes filled with water and a lump came up in her throat. She fished in her pockets for a hanky, and then remembered it was Grandad's cardigan. Her fingers closed on something soft and silky. "Grandad won't mind my using his hanky," Mandy thought, and she pulled it out.

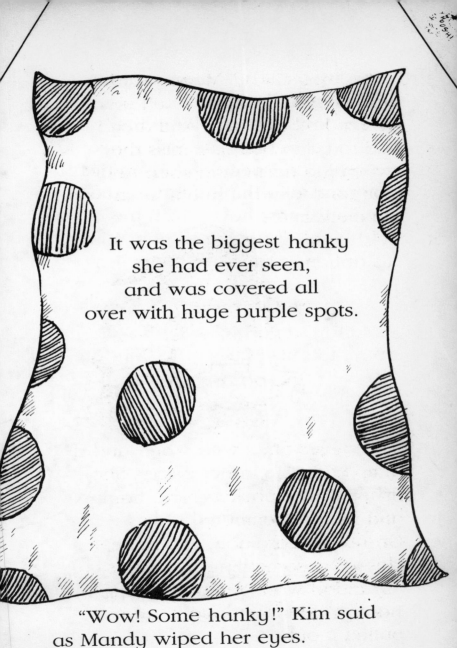

It was the biggest hanky
she had ever seen,
and was covered all
over with huge purple spots.

"Wow! Some hanky!" Kim said
as Mandy wiped her eyes.

Ian was still brooding over the way that colds spread.

"You can't really blame me," he said, "Not really. After all, if people do give other people colds, which I don't actually think they do, then someone must have given me my cold before I gave it to you, so if it's anyone's fault, it's theirs, isn't it?"

Mandy's head felt as if it was about to burst. She turned on Ian.

You go on and on and on about things, why don't you just SHU U

Kevin stared at her.

You don't need to snap, he was only explaining.

"I'm NOT!" Mandy said, and began to cry. She didn't want to, but she couldn't stop the tears running down her cheeks. The others looked at each other, and shuffled their feet.

"Maybe we'd better go," Ian said. He got up, and Kevin and Kim followed him. Buster licked Mandy's knee.

"Call yourself friends," Mandy sobbed as they trailed towards the door. "None of you wants to talk to me – only Buster cares!" And she went on crying.

"We'll come back tomorrow," Kim said. She was feeling very uncomfortable and wasn't sure what to do. Kevin and Ian hurried out through the front door without even saying goodbye, and Kim went after them. When they were outside on the path they stood and stared at the fence and didn't know what to say to each other.

"You did go on a bit," Kim said finally.

"I didn't." Ian glared at her.

"He always does," said Kevin, which didn't help at all.

"didn't"

"did"

Inside the house Mandy blew her
nose hard, but the sobs kept on
coming. The door opened, and
Josie sidled in.

"What you crying for?" she
demanded. "And where are the
others?" She sat down on the sofa.

Mandy couldn't bear it.
"Go away!" she shouted, waving
the purple spotted hanky at Josie.
"Go away! You're always hanging
around!"

Josie began to sneeze.

AATISHOO

She sneezed sixteen times,

atishoo ATISHOO atishoo Atishoo
atishoo ATISHOO ATISHOO ATISHO
Atishoo ATISHOO ATISHOO atishoo
Atishoo ATISHOO ATISHOO
and on the sixteenth sneeze she blew herself right up the chimn
Atishoo

ATISHOO

Mandy was left open-mouthed
gazing at the empty space where
Josie had been – but wasn't any
more.

Mandy's mum put her head
round the door. "Did you call?" she
asked. Mandy shook her head. She
couldn't say anything.

"That's all right, then. I'll bring
you a drink later."
Her mum disappeared,
but through the door
in the usual way.

"Josie?" Mandy called up the chimney, very softly. There was no answer. "Josie? Are you there?"

There was a faint muffled squawk. Mandy rushed to he window and peered out to see if the rest of the gang were still around. They were wandering slowly down the path, and seemed to be arguing.

Mandy pushed the window open.

KIM, KEV, IAN! QUICK! YOU'VE GOT TO HELP ME!

Kevin turned round, while Ian and Kim went on waving their arms and shouting at each other. Mandy beckoned wildly, and he came slowly back towards her.

"PLEASE!" Mandy said. "Come back! Josie's gone up the chimney, and I don't know what to do!"

Kevin was about to say ha ha, very funny, but Mandy looked so frantic that he took a step closer.

"Swear?" he said.

Mandy drew her finger across her throat. "On my bones and blood! She's up the chimney – I heard her! We've GOT to get her down – Mum'll kill me if we don't!"

"KEV! Are you coming?" Ian and Kim were waiting for him on the pavement.

"Come back! We've got an emergency!" Kevin shouted.

"SSSH!" Mandy glanced behind her at the door, but there was no sign of her mother.

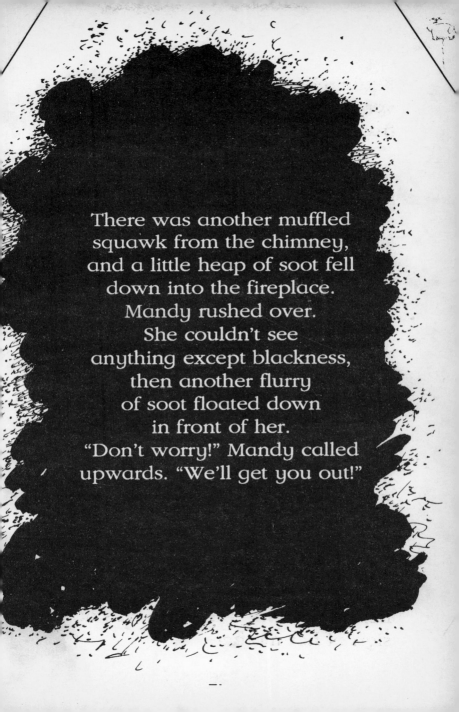

There was another muffled
squawk from the chimney,
and a little heap of soot fell
down into the fireplace.
Mandy rushed over.
She couldn't see
anything except blackness,
then another flurry
of soot floated down
in front of her.
"Don't worry!" Mandy called
upwards. "We'll get you out!"

Kevin leaned in through the window. "Shall we ring the doorbell?"

"NO! You'd better climb in here – my mum'll want to know what's going on if I let you in through the door."

There was a great deal of heaving and scrambling,

and a large
ripping noise.

"OW!" squealed Kim, who was
the last in. "That was my jeans."

"Sorry," said Mandy. "But
whatever are we going to do?"

"I don't see that it's anything to
do with us," Ian said stiffly. "She's
your sister."

Kevin punched him on the arm.
"Don't be mean," he said.

Kim went over to the fireplace and stared at it.

"Are you sure she's stuck?" she asked. "She might have gone right out of the top. She might be on the roof."

"But I can hear her in the chimney," Mandy said. "And soot keeps falling down."

Kevin bent down by the sooty grate.

He heaved a chair over to the
window and climbed out again.
Buster barked enthusiastically.

"Quiet, Buster!" Kevin said.
He stepped back to gaze up at the
roof, and suddenly began to wave.

"What is it? Can you see her?"
Kim leant out. Kevin gave her a
thumbs up sign, waved once more
at the roof and hurried back to the
open window.

"She's sticking out of the top," he said. "If she wriggles about a bit she could probably get out on to the roof, and then we could get her down from there." He grinned. "She's EVER so dirty."

"Does she look all right? Is she frightened?" Mandy asked.

"No – she's waving like anything. Come and see." Kevin rushed off again and Kim and Ian scrambled out of the window after him.

"What about me?" Mandy called, jumping up. No one answered. She glanced down at her nightie and bare feet, stuffed Grandad's hanky back into his cardigan pocket, shrugged her shoulders and climbed out as well. As she padded across the flowerbeds and on to the grass she noticed that her head felt quite clear.

"Must be the fresh air," she thought.

Mandy looked up. Josie, neatly
tucked into the top of the chimney
pot like an egg in an egg cup, was
waving at her. She was covered in
soot, and it was difficult to tell that
her jumper had ever been blue.

Down below Kevin, Kim and Ian
were standing in a row. Buster was
sitting beside them. Kevin was
scratching his head, and Buster
was scratching his ear.

"Well? Any ideas?" Mandy asked.

"She won't come out of the chimney pot," Kim reported. "She says she feels safe there, and she might fall off the roof."

Mandy sighed. "Maybe we'd better tell Mum."

Ian, Kim and Kevin shook their heads violently. "She'll only say our fault," they said.

"She's going to say it's my fault that Josie's so dirty," Mandy said gloomily.

Kevin was watching Josie try to catch a passing sparrow.

"She must be red hot at climbing," he said. "I could never have climbed up a chimney when I was little."

"But she didn't climb," Mandy said. "She – she sort of whooshed. She sneezed and she sneezed and she sneezed – and then blew all the way up."

The gang stared at her with the same open mouthed expression that Mandy herself had had when Josie disappeared. Then Ian snorted.

"Good story," he said. "I suppose you wished and waved a magic wand, too."

Mandy was frowning. "No – but I did say I wished she'd go away. And I flapped my hanky… That's when it happened!"

"What hanky?"

Mandy pulled the purple spotted silk hanky out of her pocket – or out of Grandad's cardigan pocket. "This one."

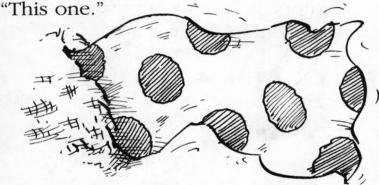

Kim and Kevin and Ian looked up at Josie, and back at Mandy. Mandy was not good at making up stories, Kevin was the best at that by far. Neither was Josie good at climbing, and she was also very fussy about her clothes. But a hanky that whooshed her up a chimney?

Kevin coughed.

"Wave it again," he said. "If it's really and truly a magic hankie and you're telling the truth, it'll work again. Wave it at me and wish I'd go away."

Ian and Kim nodded. "Go on," they said. Mandy looked doubtful.

"Suppose it sends you somewhere else? We might never find you," she said.

"OK – tell it to send me where Josie is." Kevin gritted his teeth, and shut his eyes. "Go on."

I'm ready.

Mandy shook the hankie under Kevin's nose. "I wish – I wish – I wish you'd go away where Josie is !" she said.

Kevin went on standing in the garden with his eyes shut.

"I KNEW she was fibbing," Kim said smugly. "I bet Josie climbed up but Mandy won't admit it."

There was a mad flurry of barking and a loud shriek from the top of the chimney. The gang wheeled round and stared up at the chimney pot – and saw…

Josie having her face licked by a hugely over-excited Buster.

said Ian.

said Kim.

said Kevin.

There was a silence while they
all took in what had happened.
Buster seemed perfectly happy; he
settled down on the roof beside
Josie and wagged his tail every
time she patted his head.

43

"I was telling the truth," Mandy said. "But I didn't mean Buster to go."

"If you can magic him up there," Ian said, "can't you just magic him back? With Josie?"

"Yes – of course!" Kevin sounded very pleased. "Go on, Mandy – he might fall off and break his legs."

Mandy flapped the hanky up and down in the general direction of the chimney.

"I wish – I wish – I wish that Buster and Josie would come back down here NOW!" she said.

Nothing happened. Mandy tried again, and then again.

Kim tried,

and Kevin tried,

and Ian tried,

but Josie and Buster stayed up on the chimney pot.

Mandy sat down on the grass.

"It's no good," she said. "They'll be up there for ever and ever if we don't tell Mum and get the fire brigade and things. I wish SOMEONE knew what to do."

There was a whoosh that knocked Kevin right over, and left **WHOOSH** Kim and Ian reeling into one another. Ian rubbed his head, and Kim rubbed her nose.

LOOK!

Kevin pointed upwards with a trembling finger.

Kim and Ian looked. There,
sitting on the very top of the roof
and right beside the chimney pot,
was Mandy. Josie was clapping her
hands and Buster was barking and
trying to lick Mandy's bare feet.

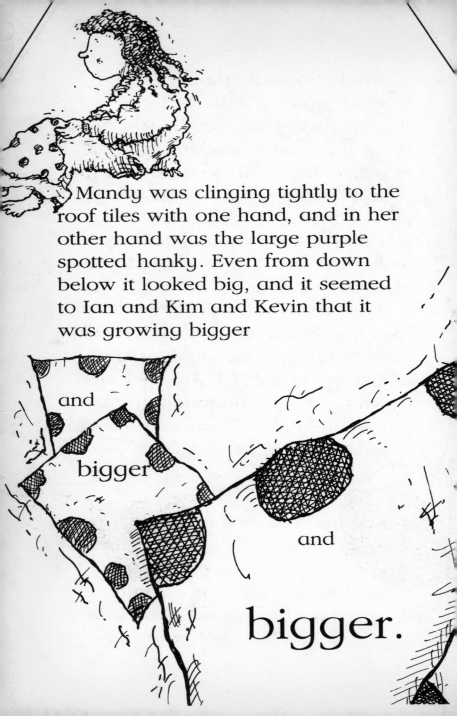

Mandy was clinging tightly to the roof tiles with one hand, and in her other hand was the large purple spotted hanky. Even from down below it looked big, and it seemed to Ian and Kim and Kevin that it was growing bigger

and

bigger

and

bigger.

Mandy, looked at it in horror.

"Have you come to fetch me down?" Josie asked, in the sort of voice she used when Mandy came to collect her from the swings in the square. "Only I quite like it up here. Can we come again?"

"I don't know," Mandy said in a wobbly voice. "I don't really know how we got here."

"You wished us, silly," Josie said. "Are you going to wish us down?" A fold of the purple hanky blew across her arm. "OH! Are we going down by magic? By magic hanky parachute? PLEASE say we are – go on, Mandy – I know we can!"

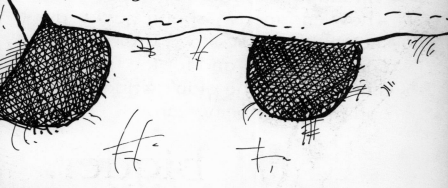

Mandy's mind was in a whirl. She didn't know why she was where she was, but the hanky must have had something to do with it. What was it that she had wished?

Mandy blinked. She had wished that someone knew what to do – and here was Josie telling her. And Josie was busy gathering up folds of the hankie, and squeezing herself out of the chimney pot. Buster let out a sharp yelp.

"You carry Buster," Josie said, "and hang on tightly!"

Mandy held on to as much of the – now enormous – spotty hanky as she could. She scooped Buster up under one arm, and for the first time in his life he didn't wriggle and protest at being carried.

"One, two, three,

JUMP"

And they did.

51

Kevin, Kim and Ian watched in open mouthed wonder as Mandy, Josie and Buster floated gently down from the roof. They reached the grass with a soft thud. As they landed the hanky floated out above them like a ceiling of purple spots. Mandy and Josie let go, and the hanky gathered itself together, shrank a little and then drifted up and up into the sky.

"I can't see it any more," Kim said, squinting into the sunshine.

"We don't need it," Josie said. "Come on – let's go home!" And she ran towards the front door. Mandy ran after her, and caught at her hand. "Sssh, Jo – Mum'll hear you if you go in that way. Let's creep back in through the window."

Josie stopped and thought about it. She wasn't allowed to climb in through windows, so she smiled and nodded her head in agreement. "OK," she said.

Kevin was patting Buster and rubbing his ears as if he hadn't seen him for months and months.

"Shall we come in with you?" Kim asked Mandy.

"If you like," Mandy said. "I don't know WHAT Mum's going to say when she sees Josie."

"Maybe we could wash her down a bit," Ian suggested, dusting leaves off the top of Josie's head.

I'm going home to give Buster his dinner, see you tomorrow.

Mandy climbed back into the sitting room, and then pulled Josie in while Kim and Ian pushed from behind.

Kim had just put her hand on the window ledge to haul herself up when Mandy's mum opened the door and came in. She was carrying a tray with a glass of orange and some biscuits on it, but when she saw Josie she screamed and dropped it on the floor.

"OH! OH! OH! WHATEVER have you been doing?" She stared and stared and stared at Josie.

Kim and Ian quietly moved away from the window, and tiptoed off across the grass. Mandy caught Kim's eye, and Kim winked and waved to her as they slipped off and round the corner.

Mandy took one look at her mum's face and her stomach tied itself up in anxious knots. However was she going to explain the state Josie was in? What was Josie going to say? If only there was some way she could distract her mum, and her think of something else.

"Mandy – WHATEVER'S been going on here? AND the window's open!" Mandy's mum closed the window with a bang, and then turned back to look at Josie all over again. "I've NEVER seen such a dirty jumper! And your HAIR!"

Josie smiled happily.

She rubbed her
fingers together
and soot floated off.

"I'm tired of being dirty," she said. "I want a bath." She looked sideways at Mandy, who was biting her finger. "Can Mandy bath me?"

Mandy jumped up off the sofa.

Mandy's mum's mouth opened wide. If she had been carrying another tray she would have dropped that one too. As it was she stared at Mandy in total disbelief.

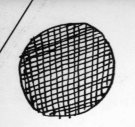

Mandy nodded urgently. Maybe she could escape after all – she grabbed Josie's hand.

"Oh yes. We'll have fun, won't we Josie?" She pulled Josie towards the door.

Mandy pushed Josie through the door and towards the stairs, pulling the cardigan off as she went.

Her mum shook her head. "I don't know," she said. "Well – all right. You'd better leave Grandad's cardigan down here, though." She shook her head again. "I'm sure there's something going on that I don't know about."

"Mum," she said, "I think I might have lost Grandad's hanky."

Her mum took the cardigan from her, and slid her hand into the pocket. "No – here it is." She straightened out the soft silky hanky, and folded it neatly into a small square.

"Wouldn't do you any harm to keep a hanky with you," she said, handing it to Mandy. "Here – you take this one. It might come in useful. Grandad's got dozens of them – he won't mind you having one for your own. Nice and soft for that sore nose. Now – go and give that child a good scrub!"

As Josie splashed happily about in the soapy water Mandy held the hankie on her lap and gazed at it. It was bright yellow, with red squares all over it...

Josie sneezed loudly. Mandy hastily put the hankie in the sleeve of her nightie, and gave Josie a paper tissue.

"I want the pretty one," Josie said indignantly. "Don't want a horrid paper one."

Mandy sighed, and passed her the red and yellow hanky.

Josie stood up very straight in the bath. She took a deep breath, and waved the hanky in the air.

"I wish Mandy would give me a bath every day," she said.

Mandy looked at her in horror, and snatched the hanky back.

"That's one wish that'll NEVER come true," she said.

Mum appeared in the doorway.

"That's better," she said approvingly. "Oh, Mandy – before I forget. I've got to go out tomorrow evening – maybe you could give Josie her bath again? It looks like she's enjoying it."

Mum disappeared, and Josie sat down in a swoosh of soapy water.

"See" she said, and grinned.